WHERE WOLVES RUN

JASON PARENT

*Hi Matt,
Thanks for having me on your show, which kicks ass!*

Jase

WHERE WOLVES RUN
Copyright © 2016 by Jason Parent
All rights reserved.

FIRST EDITION

May 2016

ISBN-10: 153343655X
ISBN-13: 978-1533436559

This book is a work of fiction. Names, characters, places, and incidents are either a product of the author's imagination or are used fictitiously, unless explicit permission was granted for use. Any resemblance to actual events, locales, or persons, living or dead, is entirely coincidental. This book or portions thereof may not be reproduced in any form without the express written permission of the publisher. The author assumes responsibility for the content of his work.

Cover Illustration by Tenebrae Studios.

WHERE WOLVES RUN

1.

KONRAD'S FATHER had been hunting the beasts since long before his birth. Father's pursuit had brought him all across Europe, from the coldest wilderness of Muscovy, to the hidden glens of the French Alps. Weary feet had at last turned toward Rattenberg. Years of traveling had brought him home.

But it was not a happy return. Their quiet house sat beyond the outskirts of the declining town, its neighboring copper and silver mines picked clean. Lost souls seeking fortunes had been lured away by new mirages, leaving behind those who had sprouted from centuries-old Bavarian roots, never caring which empire claimed them.

Theirs was a simple home, a mixture of wood, wattle, and daub providing a safe haven for Konrad and his family. He and his mother worked the land, grew more than they needed to survive, and traded the surplus. Meat came from the hunt, and, at twelve years old, Konrad had already become quite good with the bow. He hunted rabbit and deer in the surrounding forest and protected the livestock from the occasional wolf. Thin and lithely, he pranced over rock and root with the grace of those indigenous to the forest.

Mostly, he and his mother lived alone, happy. Father was away much of the year, bartering or taking odd jobs in far off places. When he stopped home, it was never long before he left on some new adventure.

Konrad did not know much about Father, nor did he care to learn—the man had been no true father to him. In all the time Father spent away, Konrad worried that he had been the reason for his father's absence, whether his father had ever loved him at all. After years of doubt and remorse, Konrad eventually stopped caring, and so died the last embers of affection he fostered for his kin.

Konrad knew as little of the world beyond his home's border as he knew for the man who had abandoned him for it. Their land sat at the southern edge of a vast wilderness, and Konrad had come to know all the wild within it. The trees were his playground, the streams his pools. He felt at home there, free from daily chores and Mother's orders.

Yet Konrad had never met or seen before the wild things that arrived on their doorstep. These beasts were worse than savage. They were evil.

When they came one night in late September, Mother seemed as though she knew what they were and why they were there. Father was away on some vague trip to mountains in the west. He had left Konrad and his mother alone to face an unspeakable brute and its cohorts in sin.

Mother shoved aside the wooden table upon which they had just finished their supper. Beneath it, the floor consisted of large flat stones arranged like puzzle pieces in dirt. The largest was irregularly shaped, nearly two meters long—hand less than a meter wide. Yanking a pickaxe from the wall, she drove it into the dirt and wedged it beneath the rock, prying it loose.

The rock covered a storage area as shallow as a coffin. "Get in," Mother urged. She propped up the slab at an angle. Howling broke the silence outside: wolves. Their haunting refrains came from all directions.

"Quickly!" Her voice was low but sharp. She pulled him close, her wet cheek smearing against his. She assisted him into the hole.

A clever but unlearned boy, Konrad did not fully understand his mother's apprehension. Still, he did as she commanded. His big brown eyes widened as his mother lowered the lid, blocking out all but a crack of the hearth's warm glow. She told him, begged him, to stay quiet no matter what he might hear. He nodded, chin quivering, knowing something was terribly wrong, his imagination filling in the details.

Shock made him keep his promise of silence. He choked up in panic as terrifying sounds, growling and pounding, came from just outside. Scratching at the walls followed. The nauseating cacophony traveled through the dirt as if to mock Konrad for his cowardice as he lay in his sarcophagus. Is that what those demonic creatures were doing? Taunting them?

If so, the taunting stopped. A moment of silence gave life to hope. It shattered as easily as the door beneath some terrible force. Konrad peeked through the crack, but his view was limited. He heard a struggle above him. His mother spoke not a word; her screams said it all.

What sounded like droplets of rain spattered upon the thin rock above him. Konrad envisioned ogres, demons, and other monsters of fables and lore come to life, come to rob him of his mother.

His bladder let go.

A great weight wobbled the lid as his mother's agony grew louder. Konrad reached up and touched his fingertips against the cold rock, wanting to help his mother, knowing he could not. He was weak, just a boy. An incomprehensible power, one he could never hope to match, loomed over him.

Or was he just too frightened to try?

A thud hit the slab, then another, hammering it closer to Konrad as it chiseled into the dirt walls around him. Flakes of earth dusted his bushy hair and soiled his clothes. Claustrophobia sent his mind whirling. The walls of his grave spun with it. He would have battered that rock, pushed it up with all his might, but his arms had lost their range of motion. He was trapped, helpless, his mother's dying screams echoing through his head.

The rock lid cracked beneath its heavy load. His mother's woolen tunic filled the creases. Her screaming ended abruptly, then silence. Her shirt ran with blood. It dripped like spilled wine into the storage area.

For a moment, Mother was still. Her body began to shake. Demons he could not see, three maybe four of them, grunted and slurped. Through the sliver-thin opening, Konrad watched as his Mother lurched skyward, lifted as though she were light as the air itself. Something stepped over the crack. He thought it was a foot, maybe a paw, but no animal he knew had nails like that: sharp talons, hawk-like but as big as knives and jutting from toes covered with black hair.

As quickly as it came, it was gone, and Mother crashed down onto the lid. Whatever it was had flipped her over. Her dead, unblinking eye stared through the crevice.

Consciousness waned. The last sounds Konrad heard before blacking out were the ravenous gorging of the animals above and the tearing of human flesh.

2.

Konrad spent two days pinned beneath rock and his mother's corpse before someone came. He had stopped scratching at the slate early on in his confinement, realizing its futility. Retched vapors wafted in from the exposed entrails rotting above. Madness seeped into his mind until it threatened to unravel.

His consciousness fleeting, he could not be certain that the footsteps he heard outside were real. His fingertips had lost all sensation. His body, shivering so much his muscles ached, craved nourishment. His mouth had gone as dry as dead leaves. But he did not cry for help, wondering if he truly deserved it, not knowing if it was help that had come.

Shoes stomped upon the dirt above. They were real, he felt certain, but to whom did they belong? Would their owner beget his salvation or ruination? Despising his own feebleness, Konrad accepted his fate.

Fear rose once again in his throat as his mother's decaying body was pulled from the rock. Had they returned for him?

Blinding light stabbed at his eyes, first through the crack, then from the world as it opened up before him. The silhouette of a man, blurry but certainly human, hovered above.

Konrad felt hands grasping his shirt. Someone called his name as he dragged Konrad from the filth—someone whose voice Konrad had once longed to hear, the person who had left him and his mother alone, defenseless, to die.

His mind darkened, his thoughts as black as oblivion. *Father.*

3.

When Konrad woke, he found himself atop his bed, washed and clothed. His father sat beside him. Everything was warm, calm. A naïve hope that the last three days had been a nightmare was beaten into obscurity by the vivid memory of his mother's final moments. Tears filled his eyes.

"Finally awake?"

The room came into focus. Konrad's father sat beside him. Shadows danced upon his father's face, the flickering light of the lantern casting mischievous black flames. Father looked old and worn, his skin like leather feuding with time. Chiseled troughs on his forehead and beside his deep-set eyes revealed the labors of his years. His ragged, unkempt beard, more gray than brown, looked like it had not been washed since the beginning of the long war. The man owning it, scarred and empty, looked as embattled as the war itself, all thirty years of it. Tissue hung upon his frame as if it had tired of shielding the skeleton beneath it.

Life had stopped favoring him years ago. He was not the man Konrad remembered, a feeble likeness, no longer worthy of Konrad's fear or reverence, if ever he had been.

"I had feared the worst," he said solemnly, fiddling with what appeared to be a cross tied around his neck. He tucked it beneath his shirt. "I checked your body, but found no bite or scratch."

His shoulders drooped, and he sagged forward on his stool, his gaze cast upon the floor. "Your mother did well, God bless her."

"Mother?"

Father shook his head. "She is at rest now."

Konrad had guessed as much, but his father's words still stung. "What were they, Father?"

"Werewolves." He spat the word. "Foul creatures . . . the Devil's answer to wicked men who serve him and the blight of the innocent to whom they spread their vile curse."

Werewolves? The word bore Konrad no meaning. The Bavarian forests had their share of wolves. Konrad had lost a piglet to one last spring. But wolves did not hunt humans in their homes. Wolves did not have paws like that he had seen.

A deep sigh passed Father's lips. "It is time you learned God's plan for us. It is time you learned your father's true purpose and, God willing, your own."

Over the next hour, Konrad listened with disdain as his father wove a tale so incredible that had Konrad not heard his mother's evisceration, he would not have believed it. His father explained that he had come from a small village north of Rattenberg, a place where good people had lived good lives, purposefully cut off from the land's politics and warfare. Their isolation, however, had led to their demise.

When the beasts came, monsters as big as those

that dwelled in nightmares, they were too few to fight them off. One by one, the villagers had disappeared, dragged into the forests under the pitiless round eye of the moon. Sometimes, torn scraps of clothing were found, but more often, the only evidence of abduction was the loud cries for help across an otherwise silent night.

"Wolves!" those who were not there would later place blame. Those who had seen the beasts and had lived to tell tales never spoke them, their dread sealing their mouths shut. Neighbor had turned his back to neighbor. They huddled behind doors of false security . . . until their time came.

Father had seen them. He had seen them pluck the limbs from his sister as easily as feathers from a bird. He had seen their primeval claws shred through his own father like a finely whetted axe through soft pine. He had seen their monstrous fangs, drooling gleaming sickles, tear out his mother's throat and their long, winding tongues lap up her blood.

Father had seen them for what they were: not quite man, not quite beast, but comprising the worst of both. They had been led by one, bigger and more sinister than the rest, the alpha among alphas, with pale yellow eyes burned into Father's memories. It was those eyes that haunted his sleep.

After the werewolves had devoured his family, Father had to learn to fend for himself. A boy not much younger than Konrad, he had fled then, but never since. Under the pretext of righteousness and duty, sometimes believing it true, he had spent the greater part of his life tracking and destroying them for no reason more complex than revenge.

Konrad understood his father's contempt. The beasts had killed his mother. He would see them dead for what they had done, even if that meant teaming with Father.

"So what do we do?" he asked.

"We kill them," his father murmured behind his wall of hands. "We keep killing them until there is none left of them or none left of us."

Father raised his head and placed a hand on his son's shoulder. Konrad shrunk away from the contact and crossed his arms.

"When do we begin?"

"As soon as you are ready." Father again looked away, his gaze bouncing from one object to another, never landing on Konrad. "We won't need to hunt them," he said softly. "As beasts, they are fearless, but they are cowards as men. They will come for us, but they will wait until the next full moon. For three nights, when the moon is fullest, their power is strongest. Only then can they change into the monsters that killed your mother. Only then will they attack."

A spark ignited within his father as he spoke. Perhaps he was not the useless old man Konrad had believed him to be. Perhaps he could avenge Mother.

"How do we kill them?"

"With silver," Father said, unsheathing a long dagger from a scabbard by his side. "It was not chance that I built my home near the mines. I have been taking what I can from them for the greater part of my life and having it forged into weapons. The Elector would have my hands if he knew what I have stolen."

He held out his hands before his face and examined them. Konrad wondered if the Elector would have done him and his mother a service had Father been caught. Father had gained his title by the mere fact of Konrad's birth. But time and absence had stripped the man of that title as easily as stewed pork from a bone.

"We have twenty-eight days to find them in their human form. We kill the man, and the beast dies with him."

"How will we know the monster if all we see is the man?"

"Our hamlet is small. Rattenberg is a shell of what it used to be. Outsiders do not pass through unnoticed. And a pack did this, likely seeking revenge for what I did to its brethren, or for what I will do if I have the chance. I have been hunting since I was your age, son. My deeds became known among their brood soon after, and the werewolves have been hunting me since. They have my scent. They have tracked me here, and they want my blood. But we shall see who is better at the hunt."

"Wait," Konrad said, his brow furrowing. An idea hit him hard and fast, difficult to process. He collapsed under its weight. "You brought them here?"

Father buried his face in his hands, a proud man broken. But Konrad had no pity for him. At that moment, the flame of hatred he carried for his father exploded into wildfire, Konrad blaming the man as much as the beasts for his mother's death.

He waited in silence. The shame that had weakened his father's resolve would lift—the man was as cold and firm as stone. Konrad was content to let it linger as long as it would. He sneered as his father bellowed out apologies he would never accept. His own tears had dried, consumed by the fire within, burning hate. He clenched his fists, his knuckles whitening. Letting out a breath, he set his jaw and numbed his sadness with quiet rage.

First, the beasts . . .

Konrad had many questions, but he kept silent and listened intently. All that mattered then was that the beasts died. He had to focus, to shift his resentment for his father's mistake to the monsters that had ravaged his mother. The more pain he and Father could inflict, the better.

"Finding the first of them," Father continued, "will be easy. When they came here and found me absent, one stayed behind. He has been watching us, reporting back to his kind. He has yet to notice the eyes I placed on him."

Konrad jumped up. He started for the door, wondering why his despicable father had not already slaughtered the man. "Where?" he asked behind gritting teeth.

"He is staying at Linhart's Inn. But be still, boy. What we must do must be done in secret. We must plan. And you must be ready. When the time comes, your hand cannot hesitate, lest you find it removed from your body."

Konrad stood tall, if tall could be measured by presence rather than stature. "I am ready."

His father snapped. "You are *not* ready! You are an impulsive boy filled with thoughts of vengeance that will only leave you buried under dirt. Do you think I charged at the werewolves that killed my parents, that ate my sister before my very eyes? I have killed many since, ten for every one they have taken from me. It would not have been so had I thrown my life away in some brash, impulsive attack."

Konrad scowled. He had heard enough talk. Who was Father to lecture, he who had failed to protect his family when they needed him most? He was a coward, a hypocrite who only failed to act so that he could save his own hide. Those who killed his mother had to be made accountable.

But the sullen voice of logic whispered inside his head. *They will kill you.* Konrad's body may have been small, but his mind's strength surpassed its age. His father was right, as bitter as admitting it tasted. Konrad closed his eyes and let the rage fester.

When his mind went cold, Konrad dissected his father's plan. "You said you saw this spy. What makes you so sure he is one of them?"

"His eyes. The beasts may appear human, but their eyes are wild, as feral as any of the creatures of the woods."

"That is all? You would condemn a man to death by the quality of his eyes?"

Father scoffed. "You will come to understand when you are face-to-face with the monster."

"How many men have you killed for having these eyes?"

His father stiffened. "I have hunted and slain dozens of beasts."

"And have you never been wrong? Have you ever killed someone who was not a werewolf?"

"Best to leave certain questions unanswered, boy." Father bore down upon Konrad, but took a deep breath before he let his fist fly. He returned to his seat.

"Besides, you will know this man's true nature without doubt. The manner in which he glared at me as I entered town . . . it was as if he were baiting me. I might have killed him then, and the town would have seen me executed for murder. Make no mistake: most of those who would witness our acts would not understand. We must be swift but also patient. Above all, we must be discreet."

Father threw his dagger. It stuck into the wall beside Konrad.

"First, you must train."

4.

THE NEXT FEW WEEKS passed quickly, Konrad spending his time learning how to wield a dagger and listening to his father ramble on about werewolf lore.

Konrad was a fast learner. He was no means a master with the weapon, but he quickly picked up the basics: how to attack, how to parry, and how to drive the point through a man's heart. Despite his youth and small frame, Konrad showed surprising strength, fueled by violent determination. What he lacked in muscle, he made up for in speed and deftness. But the physical training was meant to be precautionary; Father hoped to kill the werewolves without a fight— to kill them as humans and when they least expected it.

As far as Konrad was concerned, justice was justice no matter how served. But the second part of his training, his father's lectures, seemed pointless. If the goal was to kill them before the full moon, then what more did Konrad need to know beyond their regenerative capabilities and apparent allergy to silver? He remembered how easily his mother had been lifted, how big the beast sounded, how much power it flaunted. He shuddered. He was no match for that.

"What if I have to fight a beast?" The question came out weakly, blunted by the hideous possibilities it evoked. Father heard it.

"Then you have already lost." The gravity of his words fell hard upon Konrad's shoulders. "If you spot it before it spots you, you run, you hide, and you pray. If you are cornered and cannot escape, then you die bravely. But die you must! Never let it turn you."

Konrad stared, speechless. It was not the answer he had hoped for.

Father ran his fingers through his wiry hair. "I am sorry, Konrad. You are too young to have this misery thrust upon you. You should be out kissing girls and causing mischief, not fearing for your life."

Konrad tilted his head and threw back his shoulders. "I am not afraid."

"Then it is just as I feared: a head full of rocks." Father tapped his temple. "This is your best weapon," he said. "This is how you survive."

Konrad dismissed the insult. He *would* survive. The thought of running one of those vile creatures through brought a wicked smile to his face. If his choices were kill or be killed, logic dictated the former. His heart would guarantee he enjoyed it. He saw himself acting without hesitation, without remorse. He prayed reality would be as kind.

"I am ready."

Father grunted. "Yes, well, you are as ready as time will allow." He shook his head. "So be it. We have waited as long as we can. The full moon will be upon us two nights hence. We must do it tonight. Do you remember the plan?"

Konrad nodded.

"Then let us be off."

Konrad grabbed his coat and followed his father into the cold, late-October night. His breath rose like a specter from behind chattering tombstones. The moon shone brightly above, a sliver shy of a full circle. Konrad had always found it beautiful. That night, he looked upon it with disdain.

"Come help me with this." Father called him over to the small cart that often went with Father on his long trips. Konrad had thought he had used it to carry vegetables or livestock to trade wherever his travels brought him. Father had always returned with salt, linens, or other valuables. Konrad had a new guess as to where all the supplies came from: robbed from those his father killed or paid for in coin similarly acquired.

His father looked as if he were trying to tear off the bottom of the cart. As he approached, Konrad saw that a false bottom, an unremarkable slab of weather-worn wood, covered the true base. Beneath it rested a rusty shovel and a damp, pungent-smelling blanket, stained by the horrors it had smothered.

As they pulled the board free, Konrad struggled to support its weight. Something metallic clanged beneath it. *Chains?* He tilted the slab and peeked under it. *Shackles.* He raised an eyebrow, beginning to wonder if he knew anything of his father at all.

"Keep tilting it. I will grab the other end. We can carry it into the house sideways."

Together, they lugged the slab into the house and slid it across their table, chain-side up. Konrad tasted acid in his mouth. The board sat where he had last eaten with his mother. It hovered over where his mother had herself been eaten.

As he gawked at it, his distaste for the crude device intensified. While its flipside had been ordinary, this side conveyed a vivid history. Worse, its arrangement in their home could only mean that it would continue to serve its terrible function. Shackles were embedded into the wood at each corner. Half a meter down, another shackle sat centered. This locking clasp was big enough to fit Konrad's waist.

He gasped as its purpose became clear: it was meant to trap a beast at its neck.

The shackles were thick, heavy half circles of iron. Jagged metal shards jutted from the undersides of each mechanism. The clasps appeared sturdy enough to hold even the strongest man. But man was not their prey.

He ran his fingertips across the surface of the slab. Splintered wood stung him like a swarm of wasps. He recoiled, examining the grooves that marred the board's face.

Not grooves. Claw marks. Some seemed almost human, wider than Konrad's fingers but matching Father's. Others were as big as a bear's. All were darkly stained.

He pulled a splinter from his middle finger and squeezed beneath the puncture to dull its sting. A bubble of blood formed. It dropped onto the primitive device as if drawn to it and seeped into a dark crevice as though the board had acquired a taste for it.

This twisted table, this crude, sinful creation, was not meant to exact justice. It was meant for torment.

Konrad tried to dispel his morbid curiosity. He could not stop his gaze from returning to the scars in the wood. Many had seen this board before, and many had struggled to free themselves from it. He wondered if any had succeeded.

As if sensing his thoughts, Father stepped closer. "It will hold as long as we need it to." He placed his hand over Konrad's, together losing their fingers into the clawed canyons. "Killing a man is not always easy." Some unperceivable memory blurred his eyes. He stiffened.

"It never should be," he said, ushering Konrad outside. "Remember, this is not murder but mercy. We are freeing a soul from the beast blood contaminating its body. Let God have the man; the Devil may take back his beast."

Murder or mercy, Konrad did not care. He hopped into the cart. His father mounted Vulkan and urged his old but sturdy Oberlander into motion, Rattenberg their destination.

5.

The path into town was quiet. At the outskirts, an owl hooted until the horse and cart approached it. The bird sped off through the air, leaving the travelers alone again. Vulkan's hooves battled against the remaining silence, their cadence a dirge upon which Konrad drifted into town.

They passed the twin naves of the Gothic Church of St. Virgil, its cold marble stonework standing as solemn as a cemetery. No one held its vigil. War had taken many from the town to die upon fields they had no interest in protecting. As many structures stood empty as there were filled. The silence in the streets, the forgotten homes, the unplowed lands—all gave Rattenberg the bleak feel of being half dead.

Even the air seemed heavy, giving no levity to Konrad's thoughts. He focused on their plan, reciting it continuously in his head, steeling himself for his dangerous role.

At the start of the main road, Father brought the horse and cart to a stop beside a trader's stand. A tattered woman was busily closing up shop. The woman saw his father and pointed down the road at

Linhart's Inn. Father acknowledged this and gave Vulkan a kick as the woman hustled away.

Arriving at the inn, Father parked in a dark alleyway where the building's steep wall blocked out the moonlight. He hopped off his horse and tied Vulkan's reins around a post.

With weak knees, Konrad slid from the cart and approached his father. His feet seemed heavier with every step.

Lips pressed flat, Father grabbed his arms and shook him. "Stick to the plan. He will smell you, know you as soon as you are near him. Do not try to be clever."

Konrad nodded. His hand fell upon the dagger Father had given him, tucked beneath his belt. Taking a deep breath, he entered the inn.

"You will know him by his eyes," his father had told him. Konrad scanned the interior. The inn was more like a tavern with rooms at its far end. Their doors were closed. The werewolf could have been in any of them.

One man stood at the bar. Another sat at a table, fondling a serving girl who sprawled across his lap. A larger table in the corner hosted four more men who were playing cards. One of them, his face hidden behind a low-tipped Tyrolean hat, tipped his head politely at Konrad when he looked their way.

Father said he had come alone. Konrad studied the fat, hairy man molesting the barmaid. His face was buried in her bosom. When he came up for air, he revealed his eyes: wild, full of lust, animalistic, but altogether human. They looked Konrad's way.

"Wait your turn, boy," he said, donning a sinister

smile that highlighted his blackened teeth. "Unless you want to eat my knuckles." He shook a fist, his other one grabbing a handful of buttocks.

Konrad turned away. Black Tooth seemed cruel, but he did not strike Konrad as the werewolf type. Not that he had much to go on. He had never seen a werewolf before. Sounds and glimpses were no substitute for experience. He began to doubt the solidity of their plan.

It must be him then, he thought, staring down the back of the ragged looking tramp slouched over the bar. His hair was long but thin and oily. His breeches, naturally brown, and his shirt, browned by sweat and dirt, reeked of poverty despite a life of hard work. He looked in every way the farmer, old and feeble, not some vicious denizen of the night.

But Konrad knew the beast's power came from its curse. As a man, it was vulnerable. And this man seemed to be easy pickings, so long as Konrad had his knife.

He walked up to the bar. His confidence returned as he stood at the farmer's side. The man did not so much as turn, seemingly unaware of Konrad's presence. His hand quivered as he raised a glass to his mouth.

"This hardly seems a proper place for a boy your age."

Konrad's heart pounded against his ribcage. The voice had come from behind him. Eyes wide, he turned to face its owner. The farmer kept to his drink. The man with the low-tipped hat swaggered up to the bar.

"Your father must be worried sick," he said,

baring a cocksure grin, one incisor biting into his lower lip. His clothes were clean: a white pressed shirt covered by a close-fitting doublet and tan breeches held up by suspenders. Stubble lined his jaw. His skin was smooth, pox-free, tell-tale signs of an easy life. Tall and lanky, with sandy blond hair, he had an air of royalty. But his clothes suggested a tradesman, or a barber perhaps, the dirt beneath his fingernails the only contradiction.

The brim of his cap cast a shadow over his eyes. He raised it.

Konrad gasped. He gazed into orbs that swirled with combative colors. Emerald green, beautiful yet mysterious, was the dominant shade. But with each flicker of the lantern, a pale and sickly yellow spiraled through those eyes like worms curling up to die. Certain virility resided in those eyes, though— something dreadfully alive.

Konrad gulped. He had found whom he sought.

His resolve fled through his pores and his armpits dampened. His hands, too, felt clammy. Konrad wiped them on his pants. His fingers twitched. He could feel his lips trembling.

The man leaned into the bar. Konrad stumbled backward, knocking into the farmer. The beer in his glass swished but did not spill. He grunted, downed the drink, tossed a coin onto the counter, and stumbled toward the door.

The bartender, a short, stocky fellow with a crooked nose, snagged the coin and stuck it in his apron pocket. He glared at the man with the cap as if he were disgusted by the mere sight of him. Did he know the man's true nature? Konrad hoped he had found an ally. He needed one.

"Beer," the man-beast said. "Make that two." He turned to Konrad and winked. "Your father need not know. Where is he, by the way? Surely he has not sent you in here alone."

"You . . ." Konrad began, his voice failing him. He tried again, but the words refused to form.

"Joren," he said, patting Konrad on the back. "At your service." He laughed heartily, full of mirth. He sounded friendly, but there was a hint of malevolence in his tone, something frightening beneath his smile. And those eyes—

Konrad sucked in air. He tried to remember the plan, but hate and fear clouded his mind. "You killed my mother," he managed at last, his voice louder than he had intended. The bartender's forehead creased when he returned with the drinks. But he skirted away, leaving Konrad and his company to their beers.

He was alone, a boy against a savage, one of the very fiends who had murdered the only person he had loved.

Joren exaggerated a frown. "Now that is not a nice thing to say. And after I just bought you a drink?" His voice was slippery, hissing like a snake. Even in human form, the creature had fangs.

Konrad's blood boiled. Joren's casual dismissal of his crime sizzled like fat in a skillet. If only he had fangs and claws, Konrad would have torn Joren to shreds.

"You will be damned for what you did," he said, the words spitting through clenched teeth. He opened his coat, showing off his dagger. "Your time has come."

The yellow of Joren's eyes burned like torches. He stared at Konrad with all the heat and intensity of an inferno. He fell silent. His humor left him.

Konrad froze. The tension between them rose with the anger welling inside him. Every gram of his being yearned to stab Joren, right then, right there. He had yet to find the courage to draw his blade. His fingers coiled around the hilt of his dagger. His courage would come sooner than later.

"There will be no trouble in here," the bartender said. "You both should leave."

Konrad broke from Joren's hypnotic gaze. He had not noticed the bartender approach.

Joren's smug grin returned. He flashed it at the bartender and downed his beer.

Konrad's beer remained untouched. He scoffed at Joren and headed for the door, hoping the man-beast would take the bait. If Father followed through with his part in their risky scheme, maybe, just maybe, Konrad would not end up food for mongrels.

Joren followed. Konrad heard his boots clomping upon the floor behind him. He stepped into the brisk night air, a brutal killer trailing at his heels.

"Here is the first and last lesson I will ever teach you," Joren began. "Never turn your back to someone you accuse—"

His words were cut off by the sound of metal against bone. Konrad turned in time to see Joren falling to the ground, unconscious before he hit the dirt. Father stood over him, a shovel ringing like a tuning fork in his hands.

"Help me lift him," he said. Konrad hurried over. The street was empty, but the night was young.

Passers-by were likely. They had to get Joren into the cart quickly.

Father ran to the cart and threw the shovel into it. He hustled back to Konrad, who had lifted Joren to a sitting position. They raised the unconscious man to his feet. Father slung him over his shoulder, carried him to the cart, and dumped him in with all the delicacy the beasts had shown Konrad's mother.

They covered Joren with the blanket. Konrad hopped in beside him, while his father untied Vulkan. Without another word, they stole away from the inn.

6.

FATHER DROVE poor Vulkan as fast as he could over the uneven terrain between Rattenberg and home. The cart creaked and jolted over every bump, threatening to break apart. But it held fast, and they made it home without incident.

As it turned out, they had little time to spare. A moan resonated through the blanket. The man beneath it stirred.

"Quickly," Father said, as he came around to the back of the cart. "We must bind him before he wakes."

Konrad jumped out. He and his father each grabbed one of Joren's arms and yanked him from the cart. They dragged him into the house, his boots carving lines in the dirt.

"What?" Joren muttered, dazed and drooling. His hat was missing. Blood matted his hair, only partially concealing the shovel-made gash.

They pulled Joren next to the table. Father released his arm. Joren's face smashed into the floor. Another moan trickled from his throat, and he started to cough. Konrad propped him against a table leg, while Father circled the board, making sure all clasps were open.

When he finished, Father helped Konrad roll Joren onto the table. They pushed him into its center. Joren's eyes were open now, glossy and rolling. His moans grew louder.

"I will secure his neck first," Father said. He lifted Joren's head, positioned it over the open arms of the clasp and dropped it between them. Joren's head hit the wood with a thud. He winced, and his head rocked from side-to-side, but his eyes filled with consciousness.

Father clasped the first shackle under Joren's chin. It was too large to hold him, the metal spikes on its underside several centimeters away from Joren's skin. Konrad was sure he could slide out of it. The shackles were meant to pin down a larger captive. If they waited a couple of days, perhaps they would have their chance.

Joren's eyes opened wider. He seemed alert. Still, he did not resist. Father easily tugged his limp left arm toward the clasp in the board's top-right corner and slammed it shut. Joren lurched. His face reddened, the veins in his temples pulsating while his eyes bulged from their sockets. From his mouth came a breathless wheeze. He tried to sit up. Then he screamed. The jagged pieces of metal stabbed at his wrist and neck as he struggled to free himself.

"Ball this up," Father said, handing Konrad an unwashed rag. "Shove it into his mouth and hold it there until he quiets. Though the curse should be dormant now, it is safer not to let him bite you."

The need for silence seemed dubious, their

nearest neighbor several kilometers away. Still, Konrad followed his father's orders without question. He did not want to hear Joren speak. He cared not for filth spewed from the mouth of an animal.

As he shoved the cloth into Joren's mouth, his eyes met the man-beast's. Joren's irises were mostly yellow now, whirlpools of energy and awareness. His gaze was furtive, trying to comprehend his surroundings, no doubt. He gnashed at Konrad's fingers and spat out the rag. Konrad forced it back in, only to have it spat out again. When Father drove his elbow into the bridge of Joren's nose, the struggle was over.

"Never mind that now," his father said. Blood gushed from Joren's nostrils. "He will not be able to breathe if we gag him. We do not want him to choke . . . not yet, at least. He will be quieter now."

It was true. Joren's screaming and growling were replaced by coughing, spitting, and gurgling. But he thrashed fiercely as Father bound his right wrist, and he kicked feverishly as Konrad and his father secured each leg. Joren's efforts only cost him additional suffering. His flesh was torn at the neck, wrists, and shins by the shackles' barbaric underbellies.

With Joren bound, Konrad looked to his father for guidance. The malice in Father's eyes told him that Joren's suffering was only beginning. Father wanted to find the rest of the pack. He needed Joren alive. Since Joren had been given the menial task of spying on them, he was likely the runt of the litter. Yes, he probably dined on scraps of Konrad's mother, but it would have been the alpha that savored the kill and fed on the choicest bits. And although they would have long since been digested, nothing would stop Father from trying to cut them out.

They had less than two days to find the pack, if Father's calculations could be trusted. Once the moon rose two nights hence, full and fat, the pack would turn. It would come for them. Father set to work.

Fortunately, Father needed little more than an hour to obtain the information he sought. A bucket filled with parts served as a testament to his grit. Konrad stared at that bucket, horrified into silence by the ghastly mutilations he had witnessed. Most of Joren's fingernails, pried loose by Father's dagger, now resided in the bucket. A few were still attached to fingers. A couple of toes, several teeth, and most of an ear completed the collection.

Father never flinched.

An eye had been next for the bucket, but Joren betrayed his comrades before that could happen. Konrad was thankful for it. His stomach had weakened to a point where vomit threatened to rise at the mere mention of another cut. Halfway into the torture, he had looked away, no longer caring if his father thought him frail.

"They are in a cave," Joren blurted, blood from toothless gums spouting as he spoke. "Less than a day's ride north of here. The river bends at their location. The shore is rocky, smooth flat rocks that lead up to the cave. They are there, I swear it. Follow the river, and you will find them."

"I know the place," Father said. He rose and exited the house.

When he returned, he was holding what looked like a smaller version of Vulkan's bridle. He jammed its bit into Joren's mouth, the tortured man too weak to protest. When Father fastened it around Joren's head, Konrad could see that it had been crafted for that very purpose. *Another of Father's wicked designs?*

"Keep him alive," Father said, kneeling before his son. "If he is lying, I will be back for that eye. But son, listen to me carefully. Do not talk to him. Do not unchain any part of him. Do not pity him. He will show you none if given the opportunity. Only evil men choose to live with this curse."

Father stood. "If I am not back by dusk on the second day, drive your dagger through his heart. Do not wait for nightfall. Be strong, my son." He stank of blood and musk as he leaned in to kiss Konrad's head. "We do this for your mother."

He walked out the door, leaving his son to fend for himself. Konrad crept over to his bed and passed out.

7.

FATHER SHIVERED. Frost prickled his skin, while the wind beat it raw. Yet it was not the cold that made his body tremble. The thought of leaving his only son with that spawn of Satan, chained though it may have been, battered his conscience. The world was a terrible place, filled with horrors that prowled in shadow. Konrad was learning it quickly, but he still had a lot to learn about evil.

Be strong, my boy.

It was *for* Konrad that he left. Should the werewolves come, a near certainty, he and Konrad would be lambs for the slaughter. Father had to reach the pack first. He had to slay them while they were yet men.

He rode until his legs ached. Then he rode until they bruised. Only when Vulkan's breath had run out did Father stop his mad gallop. Following the muddy river bank for kilometers on end was proving more than the horse could manage. Still, Vulkan carried on. He did not falter. Father could not have asked for a more faithful, fearless steed.

The sun's warm glow sparkled over the eastern

tree line when Father finally halted. He led Vulkan to the river and waited impatiently for the horse to drink his fill. He wanted to press on, to do his righteous work—the Lord's good work—and be home before Konrad had to do the same alone, a burden thrust upon him by the fate or folly of a foolish old man.

Pushing Vulkan beyond the animal's limits would have done more harm than good, he knew. Like all life, the horse was a victim to its biological limitations. Father could not make run that which could no longer walk. Should he succeed in driving Vulkan without compassion all the way to the cave's mouth, his mount would never accomplish the trip home.

Not in time.

Father hobbled the horse in the shade of the tall grass, a bed softer than hay. Within moments, Vulkan slept like the dead.

And should I fail? Father forced himself to consider the possibility. He rested beside Vulkan, nibbling on some jerky despite having no appetite. *God be with me,* he prayed. He closed his eyes.

But Father did not sleep. His thoughts plagued him, an insatiable succubus, depriving him of sleep since that day he had first fled the beasts, the day he had failed to avenge his family. Those savages had robbed him of one family. Now they sought to claim another. They had succeeded in taking his wife. They would not have his son.

Enough of this. I must be off. Father leapt to his feet. Barely an hour had passed since he had offered Vulkan a reprieve. His sudden movement startled the horse awake.

"Good. You are up. I am sorry to wake you, old friend, but we must continue on." He urged Vulkan to his feet. "Up, Vulkan. The cave is not much further. I will let you rest then, I promise."

Father glanced at the sun. *Time is yet on our side.* He estimated five, perhaps six, more hours of hard riding. The last leg of the trip would be on foot. Even in their human form, the man-beasts had heightened senses. He would need all his stealth to find the camp without being seen . . . or smelled.

And if the pack is not where Joren said it would be? Another possibility Father forced himself to consider. He shook his head. His hands shook on their own accord.

Then all would be lost.

Father gritted his teeth. Relying on a devil not to lie was a fool's mistake. It left a sour taste in his mouth. The stakes were high, though, and his options were limited. Joren's deception would bring death. Konrad would die, while Father wandered aimlessly in the woods, too far away to protect his son.

He prayed to God he could rely on the Devil, if only just this once.

8.

WHEN KONRAD WOKE, the sun beat in through the window. Ignoring his fear—and the man chained to his table—he went about his day as if it were any other. Outside was beautiful and bright, warm for October. But a storm raged within Konrad. He tended to the livestock and his other chores, going through routine as he fought against the darkness.

In the late afternoon, he hunted, his favorite pastime. He snagged a fine rabbit, which he skinned and cooked for dinner out in the field. Remembering his unwanted houseguest, Konrad imagined himself tearing into the rabbit while its heart pumped warm blood into his mouth.

He returned home with leftovers. Joren watched him as he entered. He stared down his broken nose as Konrad unloaded his kill.

Konrad avoided his gaze, but he could feel those yellow spiraling eyes upon him. They delved through his illusion of bravery, penetrating to the depths of his fear. As he propped his bow and quiver against the wall, his legs began to tremble, losing their strength. *They are just eyes*, he lied to himself. But he could not deny their power over him.

Father said to keep him alive, Konrad remembered. *But only for another day.*

He approached his prisoner. Those yellow eyes followed his every move. He examined the stubs where Joren's pinky and ring finger had been. Black striations spread from the nubs into the hand. His unblemished parts had gone milky pale.

He will need his strength to fight off sickness. Konrad glanced at the remains of the rabbit, a meaty thigh he had intended to place in a stew. *What if he tricked father, and I need to keep him alive longer?*

"Are you hungry?"

Joren nodded. The bit scraped against his remaining teeth.

"I will remove the bit, but do not speak to me," Konrad warned, trying to sound like Father. "Do not try to bite me either. I will kill you if I have to."

Joren nodded again. Konrad stepped closer. He loosened the straps around Joren's head and slid the bit onto his chin. Joren drew in a deep breath but did not speak.

Konrad retrieved the charred rabbit. He carried it to Joren and held the hindquarter over his mouth. Joren hesitated, then took a large bite. His eyes rolled back into his head, a look of ecstasy washing over him as if the rabbit were the best thing he had ever tasted. Red streamlets ran down the tender meat, Joren's gums leaking grotesquely. Konrad wondered how he could manage the pain as Joren went back for more.

When Joren had eaten as much as Konrad would chance, his fingers moving ever closer to chomping teeth, he withdrew what little food remained. He tossed the leg into the bucket that still held pieces of Joren. "I will fetch some water," he said, heading outside to the well.

As soon as Konrad returned with a full pail, Joren broke his first rule. He spoke.

"Your father is mad," he said. "You must see this."

"Shut up!" Konrad shouted, losing all composure. With so few words, Joren had nurtured a seed of doubt festering in his subconscious. The bucket sloshed in his hands, shaking with anger. Waves splashed over the lip.

"You are a cruel, twisted monster. You deserve everything that has happened and will happen to you for what you did to my mother."

His tears fell freely. Konrad wiped them on his sleeve.

"Konrad? That is your name, is it not? I did not hurt your mother. What cause would I have to hurt her? I do not know her."

"Liar!" Konrad had heard enough. Spit seethed between the cracks of his snarling teeth. He charged at Joren.

"Wait," Joren sputtered. "Listen—"

But Konrad was already atop him, his thighs straddling Joren's chest. He upended the bucket, dumping its frigid contents all over Joren's face.

Joren gasped. A sudden deluge rushed down his throat. Water dribbled from the corners of his mouth.

Konrad tossed the bucket aside. He seized upon Joren's confusion and jammed the bit back into his mouth. Joren squirmed, but Konrad was too quick. He drew the straps tight before Joren could tell another lie.

And they were lies. They had to be. Father had done awful things to this man, terrible things of which Konrad, even with all his misgivings toward his father, would not have believed him capable a month prior. But Father's cause was just, virtuous even. Violent crimes called for violent retribution. Brutes deserved no benevolence.

But werewolves? Creatures that were half-man, half-beast?

It did sound mad. Konrad had not seen what had killed his mother. He had caught of glimpse of something furry and big, not necessarily unnatural. He had heard enough to know them wicked beasts, but perhaps his terror had transformed them from animals into monsters. Bears, with their broad jaws and massive claws, could have ripped his mother apart as easily as a loaf of bread.

No, he scolded himself. He scowled at Joren. "You *are* a monster. Your death cannot come soon enough."

He leapt from the table and got into bed where he sobbed quietly, wishing Father were there, wishing he had not left him alone with their captive. He was a farmer's son and had known nothing of the darkness. And dark actions bred darkness within him. It begged for retribution.

Why had his father failed to prepare him for these creatures? Why was his mother the only one willing to sacrifice herself so that he might live? All that had occurred — Mother's death, the demons now hunting Konrad, all his fear and suffering — had been his father's doing. And the bastard was not even there to see it through.

Konrad buried his face in his hands, afraid of the way his life had so abruptly changed, horrified of what he might be becoming: his father—not that frigid, absent man he had known most of his life, but the sadistic torturer who chopped off fingers and toes as if doing so were as natural as the grass and rivers and forests of the daylight world, a world without nightmares.

Konrad closed his eyes. Hours passed before he drifted to sleep, paving the way for the nightmares to come.

9.

THE TREK WAS LONGER than Father had remembered it to be. The sun was already low in the sky. Perhaps the years had made him slower.

Keeping downwind of his prey, Father crawled toward the camp. He slithered through the scrub on legs and forearms. Insects skirted from his path. Dead leaves and fallen needles gave way to his movement. Tree roots were more stubborn. They tangled into his clothes, poking holes in his sleeves and tearing his breeches.

I must stay hidden. Father scurried toward a bush still ripe with life despite the lateness of the season. He forced himself beneath its confining branches. There, in the spaces between green arteries and brown veins, Father spied upon his enemies.

"Will you stop splashing?" a burly, shirtless man asked. His trousers were rolled up to his knees as he waded in the river. A long, wooden rod jutted over his shoulder. His broad, muscular back faced Father, its girth boding trouble.

"You are scaring away the fish."

A golden-haired lass cackled loudly as she bathed

farther away from shore. She wore nothing but the hair under her pits and on her legs, the thickest patch growing where those legs met. Father felt winter's bite, and he was dry. He could not comprehend how the woman could withstand such cold. She actually seemed to be enjoying it.

"What fish?" she asked, still laughing. "There are no fish here. They have all gone to sleep where only they know, but they shall return long after the snow." She sang the last bit, ending with a snort and a chortle as she splashed her companion.

The shirtless man ignored her. He kept on spear fishing. Every so often, he would thrust his pole at something beneath the water, but if it was a fish, the man could not catch it.

The woman slapped the water, then crossed her arms. She cocked her head at the man who paid her no attention. Then she waded closer.

"Why do you waste your time with that? The moon will soon be full and bright. Oh, how we will feast then!" She raised her arms at the sky, twirling and laughing, as giddy as a little girl. "There will be plenty to eat, prey with warm blood in their veins, fresh from the hunt." She slapped the water again, pouting. "Not stinky fish."

The shirtless man seemed entirely disinterested in the woman's theatrics. His head tilted downward, his gaze fixed somewhere beneath the river's cloudy surface. His shoulders lifted, and with them, the spear.

The woman would not be ignored. Her bushy eyebrows arched high upon her forehead. A wry grin wormed its way across her mouth. She sashayed toward the man without inhibition. Her fingers danced up the inside of his leg, searching and finding purchase. Deadpan, the man continued to fish.

"The trout will be dormant soon, and the moon will be as vacant as our bellies. If you must hold a rod, grab another spear and help me catch our dinner. There are more of them inside the cave."

"Humph. I will not go in there. Samuel is sleeping. You know how he can be when someone wakes him." The woman giggled. "One might think he was some kind of animal."

Her smirk widened. "Besides, I have all the rod I need right here."

"Let go, Simone."

Rejection played across the woman's face. She twisted her hand and all she held in it. The man growled. He swatted her away with his knuckles. Simone sprawled backward into the water. When she resurfaced, she was laughing again. Her lip bled at its corner.

"You cannot blame me for being feisty. The time of the hunt draws near."

"You young pups are all the same: no self-control." He turned, and as he headed out of the water, Father finally caught a glimpse of the man—all of him. Father could not believe how big he was. His feet, covered in hair, dug monstrous footprints in the mud as he emerged from the river. His legs were tree trunks, his torso and arms a whole damn tree. His chest was broad and barrel-like. A thick mat sprouted from its center and spread like eagle wings across his skin.

Though the man's frame was remarkable for its

size, his face was remarkable for other reasons. Pale, yellow eyes gleamed from spots deep-set into sockets. His teeth were so large and pointy that they might as well have been fangs, deeply rooted in a square jaw. The beast had spent years in that man. He could no longer hide its stain.

Something familiar about the man... Father did not think he had seen him before. Not in human form.

"I am going to rest," the man said. "You should do the same. We will have a long distance to travel tomorrow, and none of us will be sleeping tomorrow night. We can take the horses most of the way, then we will be on foot. If you fall behind, we will not wait for you."

"Oh, I think I will manage. I may not be as strong, but I still have half a step on old men like you, Timour." Simone leaned back into the water. Her hair spread amorphously around her. Her toes breached the surface. Kicking her legs, she backstroked away from the shallows.

"So be it," Timour murmured. With the spear resting over his shoulder, he walked directly toward Father. Father's hand crept to his waist, where he found the hilt of his dagger. He slid the blade from its scabbard and drew it in front of him. Lying on his belly, he dared not make a peep.

Timour sniffed at the air. Father's grip tensed around his dagger. But whatever scent had caught Timour's attention passed him by. Barefoot, the man-beast shambled into the cave.

Leaving Simone alone.

Without a second thought, Father rolled out from beneath the bush, rose to his feet, and sprinted to the water's edge. The riverbank afforded him no cover, exposing him to an enemy that was younger, faster, stronger: an enemy that outnumbered him three to one. *At least three.* Father ran as fast as his old legs would allow.

Simone sang as she paddled in circles, her face up to the sky, her ears underwater. *She will notice the splash, surely. There is nothing to be done about it.* Father attacked the water with the fury of the driven. The water fought back. Its resistance tripped him, and he half-fell, half-dove into the murky depths. He swam deeper and deeper, hugging the river bottom, the light above fading with every stroke. All that remained was suffocating darkness and biting cold, a chill so fierce that his mind screamed for escape.

He searched for dangling legs as his breath ran short. He circled and found them, not dangling, but planted where the water rose only as high as Simone's neck. With his knife clenched in his teeth, he frog-kicked his way toward her. His lungs begged for air, burning in his chest.

"I knew you could not resist me," Simone said as Father breached the surface. "Wait. Who—"

Her words were cut off by a cry of pain, quickly stifled by Father's free hand as he jabbed repeatedly with his other. He pushed the knife upward beneath her ribcage. What he lacked in aim he compensated with tenacity and repetition.

The water thickened around them. Simone's eyes, wide and glassy, shrieked her surprise and cried out her pain. Father found little joy in murder, though he never second-guessed it. A father's duty compelled him to act; his desire to rid the world of werewolves made it gratifying. He might have pitied the girl for who she used to be or who she might have become, but pity would not stop Father from doing what had to be done.

He slid his hand around her neck and shoved her underwater. His knife stuck into her body as though she were an oversized pin cushion. Releasing it, he joined his hands around her throat.

The woman kicked, batting Father's face and chest with her fists, but she lacked the power she would have had in her altered state.

Father choked from Simone what little breath, what little life, remained. Bubbles, remnants of her muffled screams, rose to the surface in rapid succession. After a moment, the bubbles vanished.

Simone's eyes stared blankly at the sky, all the song and giddiness strangled from them. Her hair flittered on a current. Only then did Father relax his grip.

But it was not enough.

He pulled his blade from Simone's torso and dragged her by her hair to shore. Her blood stained the water red, the last beats of her heart pumping her life away. It created a river inside a river, offshoots stretching outward like veins into a greater body.

In the shallows, Father stabbed Simone again, this time able to ensure he hit the heart. Simone gasped, or at least appeared to gasp, her lungs releasing the last bit of air inside them as Father drove his weapon's hilt hard against her body. Water thick with foam trickled from her mouth.

Satisfied that both Simone and the beast she harbored were dead, Father withdrew his blade and cleaned it in the water. The gesture was empty; he did not bother to sheath the weapon, already planning out its next victim. Tossing Simone's body onto the riverbank to rot, he headed for the cave.

Water sloshed in his boots, so he kicked them off. Barefoot, Father climbed the stony hill that led to the cave's entrance. Flat rocks, smoothed by a lost tributary, chilled his already frozen and wrinkled feet. His teeth chattered. He pressed his lips together to quiet them, but the sound echoed into his brain, rattling his nerve. Father could survive the cold and had survived worse, but one slip up with these man-beasts would prove deadly. He would not be undone by chattering teeth.

Father stopped at the entrance and listened. Amplified by the hollow tunnel, snores bombarded him from the cave like the rumbles of an earthquake. He peered through the narrow crevice that formed the cave's mouth. It was barely wide enough for someone Timour's size to slide through, but Father guessed it opened into a large cavern. He could not see more than a few meters into the darkness, but he could trace the curves of the inner walls to points where they extended outward beyond his sight in both directions.

The snoring seemed to come from everywhere, even above him. The sound bounced off the walls, making it impossible for Father to pinpoint his target. Still, he had to seize the opportunity. *A sleeping enemy is an easy kill.*

But *two* enemies were inside. *At least two*, Father thought. He marked the location of the sun. It kissed the horizon, but had not begun to melt along it. He thought about waiting for a better moment, perhaps ambushing the werewolves as they exited the cave. Then he thought back to Konrad. His heart heavy with grief, he stepped through the opening.

The air inside was cold and damp, and Father could not stop shivering. His fingers groped along the wall as he walked. The light failed him after only a few strides. He cursed under his breath, unable to make out his own fingers as he held them in front of his face. Further in, the tunnel was black as pitch. Father turned to his other senses to find his way, always mindful of the fading daylight.

He tip-toed deeper into the cave, his every step painfully slow and calculated. The wall was his only comfort; he hugged close by it, ever creeping toward what he hoped was the source of the snoring. It boomed into his ears, drowning out all other sound, even that of the water dripping from his clothes.

He raised his right foot. It fell upon solid ground. He raised his left foot. It landed softly on something, or someone, lying in front of him.

Father froze, his knee bent and his foot hovering in the air. With the slightest movements of his toes, he examined the contours of the thing that lay beneath him. It shifted. With a snort and a wheeze, the snoring stopped.

"Fuck off, Simone," a gruff voice murmured. A hand slapped away Father's foot. Father kept it aloft, afraid to have it touch the voice's owner again or make a sound that would disturb him. The balancing act was wearying. After a few seconds, the snoring resumed.

Father released his breath in a long, quiet sigh.

This must be Samuel. He tucked his left foot behind his right. His muscles remained tense, ready for action. His dagger felt light again in his hand. If it wanted blood, Father was compelled to oblige it.

With a dancer's grace, he straddled the sleeping individual. Interlocking his fingers around the hilt, Father plunged the weapon's point into where he guessed Samuel's heart might be. A shrill howl rose from his victim. Unseen hands grabbed at his own, only to be stabbed again and again whenever they interfered with the work of Father's dagger. Eyes shot open, their wild sheen glistening in the dark only to close a moment later.

Father saw them. He adjusted his aim accordingly. The man-beast below him bucked and screamed, then fell silent. Father continued to stab. The eyes did not open again.

Bright sparks flashed before Father's eyes as his head whipped to the side. Someone else was there, someone who had hit him hard enough to scramble his thoughts. He rolled with the strike, his momentum keeping him rolling deeper into the cave, into the black. Father had enough wits remaining to know he was in danger. He stayed low and silent, out of sight. His dagger stayed behind, lodged inside Samuel's corpse.

Father shielded his face with his arms. It was all he could do to fend off an unseen foe.

Just then, he caught a glimpse of a shadowy figure rising from the abyss. It blotted out the dwindling light from the cave's entrance, standing between Father and his only means of escape.

Standing tall.

Eyes with the same sheen as the demon Father had just slaughtered, but having a ferocity to them the likes of which Father had never before seen in all his years hunting, not since before he was a hunter—*the eyes that plague my sleep*—stared straight at him from an arm's length higher than his own. Could the beast see him, even in its human form?

"You killed him," the tall man said flatly, unblinking. Father recognized the voice as that of the muscular brute he had seen outside. *Timour*.

Father kept silent. He shifted on his feet, watching to see if Timour's eyes followed him. He came to no conclusion; those sinister eyes seemed to be looking everywhere at once.

"And Simone?"

Father crouched. He offered no response.

"You need not answer. I can smell her blood upon you."

Father circled slowly toward the cave's mouth. Timour's gaze followed. He raised his nose and sniffed at the air. Then he began to laugh.

"That is not all I smell, hunter. I smell a frightened little boy who ran away from his village all those years ago. That village is gone now, but what fun it was in its final years. So many playthings, like your baby sister. I smell *you*, hunter. I *made* you."

What? A peculiar allegation, but Father was too old and practiced to be slain by cheap tricks. He kept calm, though his mind transported him back to that beast-torn village and its ill-fated souls. He remembered that day in vivid detail, the day a pack of werewolves had feasted upon his family while he hid behind a false wall, helpless—weak. He watched them, did nothing to stop them from rending meat from bone, then bone from frame. One of them, the biggest of their brood, had seemed to sense his presence, staring long at the wall while Father shook in terror. Its eyes glimmering, twinkling pale yellow, laughed at his weakness.

Eyes like those Timour brandished now.

It cannot be.

The strangers who had come to town with tongues as diverse among themselves as they were to the natives, who dwelled among the good folk and were accepted—Father long suspected them of having brokered deals with the Fallen One. When the beasts attacked, they were always absent. Never did one of their ilk meet his end. Never did one pack up and leave. Yet Father's home had not been their home. It was not their brothers and sisters who had vanished in the night.

Could this Timour possibly have been one of them? Another look at those eyes was all Father needed to convince his mind what his heart already knew to be true.

An overwhelming sadness, long since repressed, surfaced and reminded him that it had always been there. "Impossible," he whispered, knowing he had foolishly relinquished his position.

Timour bellowed with laughter. The sound filled the cave, blocking out all else. Father covered his ears. He stood motionless, trying to comprehend life's circular pattern and how he'd fallen victim to it.

"How does it feel to be hunted, hunter?"

"It cannot be. *You* cannot be. That was decades ago."

"We live by the moon, hunter. I have fed on hundreds since then. Your pitiful notions of time, your laws of mortality, are principles meant for a weaker species. We are your superiors in every way. We are your gods. You should have learned that when you were just a whelp. You will learn it soon enough."

Timour turned and dashed away. "But your son shall learn it first," he yelled over his shoulder.

His mind clouded, Father gave chase. In his haste, he left behind his only weapon. But Timour was stronger and faster than Father had ever been. Outside the cave, he watched as the man-beast bounded upon a horse and rode away, his steed kicking up clouds of dust and dirt in its wake.

He is getting away. He is after my son! Father's frenzied mind grappled for solutions. Another horse, a speckled palfrey of a similar breed to that Timour had taken, grazed in a nearby field. Father guessed it had belonged to one of the recently deceased. A saddle sat across its back. Father grabbed the horse's bridle and it jerked, but Father held it close. He climbed atop and kicked the animal hard in its sides.

The horse burst forward. Like Timour's palfrey, it too was bred for riding. Speedy it was, but durable it was not. Neither his horse nor Timour's would make half the distance in a single ride, whipped on as they were by their merciless masters.

As he galloped after Timour, Father slowly came to realize his error. Chasing after the man-beast with that unreliable steed, a mount that could fail him or fling him without warning, was a gamble at best. He needed a trustier horse, one that would overtake

Timour when his horse failed him. He doubled back for Vulkan.

Father might have smiled when he came across his old friend exactly where he had left him by the river a kilometer south of the werewolves' camp. But his worry for his son twisted his face into a constant grimace. Father stroked his faithful steed between his eyes. Vulkan leaned into his hand.

"I have to ask more of you, my friend. One more difficult ride. For Konrad."

The sun was but an ant hill crumbling in the west. Father checked his supplies and found them lacking. It seemed a lifetime since his supply of silver—arrowheads and crossbow bolts laced with the metal, sturdy pikes and swords forged with silver tips, daggers aplenty—was never-ending, plucked from a mine gorged with the precious ore. Father had done well to stockpile what he could, but the mine dried out and the metal was never all that durable. Points dulled or broke; others missed their mark and were lost.

Now, the last of his stash was jammed in a dead monster and tucked within his son's belt. Father had nothing but the cross around his neck, a small emblem of his faith only a few centimeters long. It was no weapon.

As the sun set, so did Father's chances of picking up Timour's trail. With no means to fight or follow, he journeyed along the river toward home.

10.

Konrad rose early the next morning. Lingering dreams filled with fangs and mutilation left him sullen and anxious. He rubbed his eyes. The room was empty except for Joren, whose snores whistled through his nostrils. His father had not returned.

He still has hours before he is due back, he thought, trying to calm his fears with the blandness of rationality. Sunset was many hours off. The full moon would rise in due course, no sooner.

Konrad passed his prisoner on his way out of the house. Joren's breathing had gone silent, still as the dead. Konrad was content enough that the man-beast's eyes were closed, those shimmering golden orbs that worked their feral nature into Konrad's soul. God, how he hated those eyes! Just then, he wished Father had cut them out.

As he went about his tasks, Konrad's thoughts were always upon that revolving ball of fire the sky. It rose too high, too quickly. He plodded along methodically, willing his father's speedy return. His mind conjured disturbing images of what he would have to do should Father not return before dusk.

His dagger hung heavy at his hip. Sheathed in leather, the silver blade hid untarnished, at least not by Konrad. He loathed the thought of using it and wondered how many times it had already been used.

Revenge was a universal desire. But enacting it, murdering someone, was a man's game. As much as Konrad liked to think himself grown up, his father was right: his growing had some growing to do. More than ever, he felt like a boy, scared of what he must do and terrified of the consequences should he fail to do it. His fate would be determined that night. The moon would make him a man, or it would make him dead.

Where have you gone, Father? Why have you abandoned me . . . again?

11.

WITHOUT LIGHT by which to search for Timour's tracks, Father allowed Vulkan to govern the pace at which they traveled throughout the night. He even permitted his eyes some rest as he sat in the saddle. He conserved his strength. Timour would never make it on his palfrey such a great distance, and even if he did, he would wait until nightfall to attack. Father would easily make it home before then. He would need all his strength to face the beast that would come for them, the man he had failed to kill.

The trail was as good as lost. His hope might as well have been. His toughest battle in a lifetime full of them was soon to come.

Father realized the constraints of the night had finally fallen away as he felt the warm rays of the rising sun tickling his face. He basked in them, eyes closed, letting Heaven's light cleanse his tormented soul. Was this what it felt like to be in the presence of his Maker? Was God Almighty calling him home?

Soon, he thought. *I will be with You soon.*

He opened his eyes and snapped Vulkan to a halt. *Perhaps it is not yet my time.* There, imprinted in the mud off to Father's right, a rider's tracks carried far off before him. The length of the stride told of a horse driven at lightning speed. The depth of the prints revealed the challenging time made of it.

The fool! So close to the river, knowing I would follow. Too close. He is running that horse into an early grave. Even Vulkan, a strong and sturdy workhorse, would have had difficulty traversing earth that soft. It was almost as if the man-beast wanted Father to catch him, or to at least know where he was heading. Father needed no tracks to tell him that. Ignoring his cautioning mind, Father prodded Vulkan onward, ever following the tracks from drier land.

By the time he came upon Timour's palfrey, the horse was as good as dead. Its leg was broken; Father wished he had the tools to put the animal out of its misery. It writhed upon the ground, unable to stand. Judging by the markings left in the mud, its rider had taken quite the tumble. Yet he was strong enough to stand and walk away from the fall. Footprints as big as Father's forearm led out of the mud and toward the tree line.

I have you. Father could taste the bitter steel tang of revenge cultivating in his saliva. He swallowed hard. *But what if I do not find him? What about my son?*

Father hung his head. He had left his son without a father too often. Mother was gone, and each was the only family the other had left. Father knew well what it was like to be a child alone in a world full of beasts. *How I could do that to my son . . .*

But he had been given a chance, and it was a far better chance than he could have wished for. He had run away once before. He would not flee a second time. God had seen fit to guide him to Timour. God would finally let him make amends for his weakness those many years ago, when he had abandoned family and friends to the bellies of beasts.

Konrad was smart. Konrad was strong. He could survive without Father for a few more hours.

But how can I best him? Even weaponless, Father could overcome his adversary, for Father was not alone. Vulkan could ride Timour down as easy as he had others like him in the past. Father would find a way to kill Timour. There were always ways to kill a man.

His mind made up, Father rode into the woods. He followed a trail of broken twigs, snapped branches and the occasional footprint. Deeper and deeper into the forest he went, veering from the pathway home.

The first hour into the woods, Father was sure he had made considerable progress. Still, the tracks carried on farther. The trees there grew closer together. They blotted out the sunlight. He looked up, expecting the find sunlight sprinkling through the trees to the east, but instead found it high above. *When did it get so high?*

The lowest limbs of massive trees clawed at Father's face. The undergrowth entangled his horse's hooves. Vulkan's gallop became a trot. The trot became a walk. Still, Father pressed on.

A low growl came from his left. Father reached for his blade, then remembered it was no longer with him. *You are a damn fool*, he scolded himself. He glanced left and saw a wolf of the common variety snarling his way. Father did not see the rest of its pack, but did not dare make the mistake of thinking it alone. The wolf snorted and turned, letting Father continue past it.

Father reached for the cross around his neck and kissed it. As the sun began its downward arc, he considered turning back. He could still make it home before sunset. But Timour would turn. He and Konrad were no match for a beast his size. So he did the only thing left for him to do: he found Timour.

Rather, Timour found him.

He sprang upon Father as he passed beneath a low hanging branch. Knocked from his horse, Father began to realize how much his desire for revenge had made him careless. *He must have smelled you coming ages ago.*

Father landed on a bed of leaves. If only they had provided a soft bed. His head slammed into the ground and his vision blurred. Blood soaked into his shirt at his shoulder. He staggered to his feet, jogging his eyes and mind back into focus.

Timour leapt onto Vulkan. Father smiled.

When Timour kicked, Vulkan bucked. He threw the man-beast off his back as though he were weightless.

Timour jumped up quickly. He glanced at Father, who was still half dazed, and took off running.

Father gave pursuit, zigzagging at first. He whistled for Vulkan to follow.

Again, Timour was too fast. In that thick underbrush, both Father and Vulkan were outmatched. The werewolf had thrown out a lure, and Father had willingly gobbled the bait. Now, he was deep in the forest with night bearing down on him. As if he were born to run through those woods,

Timour vanished in the distance, his every step bringing him closer to the coming moon.

Another hour passed before Vulkan's walk became a trot. An hour more ticked by before that trot became a gallop. In that time, dusk had settled upon the forest. Father had long ago lost Timour's trail.

That did not matter. He knew exactly where Timour was heading. He was too late to stop it.

Forgive me, son. I have failed you.

A howl echoed through the forest and shook his very bones. It boomed like Timour's laughter had in the cave, except here, no tricky acoustics aided its amplification. The howl's owner conveyed power and madness with volume and pitch that was unnatural.

Man had become beast. The beast wanted Father to know it.

His eyes filled with tears as he spurred Vulkan through the woods. He broke the tree line, hooves landing surefooted on short grass, much closer to home than he had thought himself.

Timour, the werewolf, was waiting.

The beast was monstrous, nearly as big as Vulkan. Its fangs were like swords. Its fur looked as thick as leather armor. The aberration was built for aggression, a vicious, man-eating devil. A long pink tongue drooped from the corner of its massive mouth, wide enough to bite around Father's head and take it clean off.

But with all the terror its visage evoked, the beast offered no violence. It sat on its haunches, its upper torso heaving with each breath. Its yellow eyes, dancing like candle flames, watched Father as Vulkan reared. Was the man-wolf smiling?

Father showed no fear, but Vulkan treaded backward. "Hold, old friend," Father whispered as he stroked the side of his horse's neck. He squinted at the beast, awaiting its move, readying himself for a battle he knew he could not win.

The werewolf rose. It stepped forward. But instead of charging as Father had expected, it turned and ran, straight toward Father's home.

He means for me to suffer. The thought iced Father's veins. Rage filled his brain, fueled his body. He roared as he impelled Vulkan into motion. Together, they charged straight at the beast.

Anger merged with desperation, and Father drove his horse faster. Somewhere in the darker recesses of his mind, he knew his actions were suicide. But he had to try! With a smidgeon of luck, perhaps he could slow the beast down long enough for Konrad to give up hope of his father's return and flee their home . . . just as he had escaped with his life all those years ago.

Stay alive, my boy, and fight them when the tides have changed.

Father tightened his jaw to keep it from quivering. *He will run when he sees I have not returned.* He forced himself to believe it. *He will hide. My boy will be safe. As for me, I go to his mother now.*

By God, the beast was fast! It sprinted on all fours, each paw landing with conviction, propelling it onward, a blur in the night. But driven by his tyrannical lord, Vulkan was faster. His horse bore down upon the werewolf.

The animals collided side-long. Father had hoped to run the beast down, accepting whatever fate would come to himself and his trusted friend. But the beast had seen him coming. Vulkan's momentum transferred into the monster's side, and the beast rolled with the blow out of harm's way. When it popped back onto its feet, it turned to fight.

Father had succeeded only in provoking the beast. He needed to devise a plan quickly, or he would be the briefest diversion on the hell spawn's path to Konrad. *Lead it away—*

Covering impossible grounds within a split second, the werewolf struck. Its sickle-shaped claws sliced at Vulkan's throat. Vulkan nickered and teetered onto his hind legs just in time to avoid certain death. But the claws yet tore hide. Four gashes, pinkish and fleshy like simmering bacon, streaked in parallel lines across the horse's underside.

Vulkan whinnied and went berserk. Father could not bring the horse under his control. His grip on the reigns slipped. Vulkan unseated him. He tumbled onto the wet grass.

When he rose, Father found the beast glowering over him.

And Vulkan kicking.

A sickening crunch came from the werewolf's mouth as Vulkan's back legs kicked through it. Though the impact drove the beast up, somehow the werewolf kept its footing. Its once-great fangs fell in broken shards from a mutilated, dislodged jaw. The man-beast stared, bewildered, pawing at its face as though it could somehow mold it back into its undamaged form.

It could not, Father knew, but time would. He had his first momentary advantage, but without weapons, he could not make it count.

The beast whimpered like a beaten dog, too stunned by its own fallibility to recognize that it was not yet out of danger. Vulkan kicked in circles with the spirit of the mad and their nightmarish delusions. Father dove out of the way as hooves streaked across his peripheral vision. The man-beast was not so lucky.

Vulkan's next kick connected with the werewolf's right eye. The eyeball burst into jelly. The socket crumbled like grain beneath a millstone. A huge portion of its head caved in as if it were the helm of some unlucky knight who had parried into the path of another's mace.

The werewolf reeled on its paws. Its good eye blinked. The beast fell over.

It is not dead. Father could be certain of that. He had killed enough of them to know that they always reverted to their human forms when their earthly existences had met their ends. This particular werewolf had the strength of a dozen of its kind. By sheer luck or the grace of God, Vulkan had managed to pacify it, but the beast would rejuvenate. And when it did, it would seek a satisfying revenge.

Father seized upon the idea that his good fortune, this incredible stroke of luck, was nothing short of a miracle. God-fearing men would always prevail over the Devil, he believed. If this unimaginable triumph, this victory of David over Goliath, was not proof of His existence and His glory and blessing upon those who kept the faith, what was? He kissed the cross around his neck and prayed for the means to finish the battle, once and for all.

Vulkan's hysterics had led him away from Father.

If he could calm the horse, he might be able to trample the life out of the beast. But Vulkan was crazed; he might as well have been unbroken. In his present state, the normally faithful steed was of no help to Father.

Drowning might work, but the beast was too far from the river to drag him into it. Father doubted he could tow the beast more than a meter or two without his horse's help. *Fire?* He shook his head. By the time he worked up a spark, the beast would be slurping upon his bone marrow.

As Father racked his brain for an answer, the beast twitched beside him. Sinuous tendons wove and braided, reconnecting tissue that had once been whole. Bone cemented itself together, a dark sorcery at work. The unholy creature was a little closer to reviving with every second Father wasted. Each tick of the clock brought Konrad closer to his demise.

Father scurried about in the dark, again praying for God to guide him. A large rock was the only salvation offered. The rock was big. *Too big.* It was as round as his waist and stood as tall as his knee. *Lord, give me the strength to lift it.*

On his first attempt, Father's prayers went unanswered. He crouched and tried to wrap his arms around it, but he had no leverage. The rock's thick base did not budge.

On his second attempt, he dropped to his knees and dug into the dirt beneath the boulder. He strained to lift it, and, at first, nothing happened. He tried again, and this time, the rock released from its earthen grave with a wet pop. Father rolled it onto its side and wiped his brow. He could hear insects skittering through the grass, their home disturbed. Something slender and black uncoiled and slithered out of sight.

Father stood and circled the rock. Its thickest part now stood upright. He squatted and wrapped his arms around the boulder where it began to narrow, scooping beneath the bulk of its weight. Using his legs and arms and all of his will, he lifted.

Father could hardly believe it when the rock rose in his grasp. But its weight was instantly unbearable. He moaned as he struggled to carry the infernal weapon over to where the beast lay.

Somehow, he made it. The boulder fell from his arms the moment he had reached his destination. The impact came with a nauseating squish. The werewolf's head smashed like rotten fruit beneath the tremendous force. Its twitching stopped.

When humanity did not return to the beast, Father rolled the rock off it and repeated the process. The werewolf's mashed head smeared blood and brain matter upon the rock and Father's arms. Three more times, Father raised and dropped that rock. On the fourth time, his arms gave out.

"Die, for God's sake, you filthy demon." Father cursed. He rolled the log off the shattered, flattened mess that had, at one time, comprised a human head. Blood, bone, and fur covered the ground like a mat.

His temper besting him, Father grabbed the pressed-thin remains and yanked, intending to separate head from shoulders. Making no progress, he dragged the beast's claw up to its deformed neck, gripped its finger as if it were the hilt of a blade and, using its own nails to carve into its flesh, began to saw.

After half an hour of countless curses, explosive stomping, incessant sawing, and another spine-shattering pummeling with the boulder, Father succeeded. Though the severed head could not be recognized as such, the body was once again Timour's. Father fell to the ground and laughed, raising his blood-stained hands to the Heavens in thanks.

Only then was Father certain that the beast was dead. It was over. He and his son had won.

Konrad.

Father sighed deeply. Konrad was on his own against a monster, just as Father had been. *The beast is secure. I checked those chains for faults myself. Konrad will be okay. He will forgive me when he hears what I have done.*

Victory was not victory at all if Konrad was not safe. Father stood. The events of the last two days were etched and painted into his body and clothes. He kissed his cross, knowing God was with him. God had protected him. Surely, He would see fit to protect Konrad, too.

Just in case, Father sought out his horse. He found Vulkan lying on his side, his heart pumping so fast that Father thought it might explode. He soothed him until his breathing slowed. When at long last Vulkan appeared to calm, he coaxed the horse to his feet. Slowly, gently, Father mounted his horse. Love and duty summoned them home.

12.

TWILIGHT BROUGHT WITH IT a tempestuous mind. Konrad paced in front of the house, biting his nails and clawing at his face, chanting "where is he" over and over again. He saw beasts in every elongated shadow, constant movement just beyond the corner of his eye. He could wait for Father no longer. He entered the house.

Joren was awake. Yellow eyes watched Konrad as he entered, but they were only partway open, lacking luster. A low grumble emanated from his throat, muffled by the bit. His cheeks were wet. Had he been crying?

"Mmphh," Joren grunted. His words were incoherent, faint noise without will. His face was drawn, his stare blank. Looking upon him, Konrad saw something all too familiar: fear.

"Mmphh," Joren grunted again. He tried to speak, to utter what might be his last words. Was he trying to confess?

Konrad looked upon his captive, and his hatred turned counterfeit. The burden of his task smothered the fire that had been consuming him. In Joren's face, he saw desperation, pitiful and mortal. In Joren's defeated mumbling, he heard the truth of anguish. In Joren's festering wounds, he smelled the rottenness of decay, of human agony. Even the air about him tasted foul, saturated by the sweat of a man having knowledge of his impending death.

Konrad's stomach twisted. Was it compassion that begged him to act? Though he could not free Joren, he could make his passing go as gently as he could manage, for manage he must. But he would allow the man to repent, to find forgiveness, to make peace with the Almighty. He loosened the tethers affixed to the bit.

"Please," Joren said as soon as his mouth was free. "I do not want to die."

Konrad set his jaw. He wanted to show his prisoner that, unlike his father, he still had morality. But if Joren saw it as weakness, he would have to correct him.

Calm, head down, he said, "My mother did not want to die either."

Joren sighed. He sounded like the calf Father had slaughtered one summer when it broke its leg and gave up on standing. Like that calf, Joren seemed ready to be put down.

"I did not kill your mother," he said quietly. "You are making a mistake. Your father has deceived you. I know I cannot convince you of that. But you will see now, as the sun sets, that I am nothing but a man."

He fell silent and looked away. Konrad rubbed the back his neck. Did the man inside the monster value his life so little that he would toss it away without a fight? Did he care so little for his soul? If the man were in control, he should seize the opportunity and confess his sins. At least then, perhaps he would find peace in the afterlife.

Or, was there some truth to what Joren said?

"Use this time wisely," Konrad said. "Ask the Lord for forgiveness. Confess your sins so that you may appear pure before Him."

Joren did not beg. He offered no more pleas to reason. He simply said, "I have nothing to confess."

Konrad shook his head, trying to dislodge doubt's snare. "We will see. Darkness is upon us. The moon shall rise, and you will begin to turn. I will kill you before your transformation is complete. If you are not the beast Father says you are, you will not change, and I . . . I will release you."

"Bless you, boy!" Joren exclaimed. "You are wise and merciful." He smiled widely. Laughter, nearly hysterical, burst from his belly.

Konrad watched Joren's hope returning. His doubt multiplied.

For a second time in two days, he climbed atop that gruesome table, kneeling over Joren's stomach, ready, he hoped, to end a cruel monster's life. He raised the dagger high, watching Joren intently, waiting.

The vibrant yellow of Joren's irises welled to the surface, swirling with revived vigor, the sparkle of life renewed. *Do it!* A voice inside Konrad's head screamed. *Even if Father is wrong, you cannot release him now. Finish it!*

A candle flickered as a cool draft blew through the room. The candlelight's orange glow grew and collided with expanding gloom. The last embers of the sun's rays were lost beneath a veil of black and mystery. Night had come too fast.

Konrad jumped down and paced the room as time ticked by. Joren showed no signs of transformation. Konrad could not kill a man who was not a monster.

Joren's breathing quickened. "See? The moon, and I have not changed! I am no monster. Do you see?"

Konrad stared outside the window, his gaze fixed upon that luminescent circle. There it was, low in the sky, the moon in all its glory, full and proud. As it rose, his heart sank. His father had been wrong, so horribly wrong. He was the real monster, and he had made a monster out of Konrad.

A trickle ran down his cheek. "What have we done?" he asked himself aloud. He ran to the door and yanked it open. Stars twinkled across a black expanse like tiny faeries laughing down at him and all his misguided deeds. The moon was not laughing; it stared down, all-seeing, all-knowing, a harbinger of vengeance.

Konrad fell to his knees. His sobs came uncontrolled. He pulled his dagger from its sheath and let it drop from his fingers. It fell to the ground where he was content to leave it. He had captured and tortured an innocent man. Surely, he was damned.

"What have I done?"

"You could not have known," Joren said, surprising Konrad with remarkable hearing. His own ears perked up, but he could not yet face the man he had wronged, the emblem of his shame.

"You were obeying your father's wishes as a good son should. But please, child," he said. "Unchain me so that I may tend to my injuries while there yet is time."

Still crying, Konrad leapt to his feet. "I am sorry," he muttered. He would try to right his wrongs. That first meant freeing Joren.

He kept apologizing as he worked the clasp on Joren's right wrist. He had it undone when he noticed Joren's fingers had somehow grown back. No, they had grown back longer. The nails were back, too, protruding like scythes from fingertips sprouting hair.

Konrad gasped, his lungs forgetting how to breathe. What he was seeing could not be. *The moon—*

He was shaken from his trance by Joren's wild thrashing. He bucked like an unbroken horse. The shackles rattled upon the board. The board pounded the table beneath. The sound of cracking wood split the air.

Konrad gaped in horror as the human bridle snapped against the strain of Joren's evolving features. His ears stretched into malformed triangles. They shifted upward on his head. His nose elongated, the nostrils moving up and out. His jawline narrowed but jutted outward to meet what looked like a snout. From it, fangs as sharp as honed blades dripped with drool and curled over black lips. The bit shattered within their bite.

Everywhere, clothes stretched and tore. Muscles expanded. Dense black hair covered Joren's face and body. Shackles strained but held, digging trenches into his flesh.

Joren howled and gnashed throughout his transformation. Konrad watched speechless, too amazed to look away, too terrified to move. The contortion, anatomically impossible without fiendish sorcery, was nearing completion. Only Joren's eyes remained his, but the gleam in them somehow seemed wilder, more appallingly beguiling. In them, Konrad saw only violence, rage . . . hunger.

He snapped himself free of the devil magic that had entranced him and wrapped himself around Joren's bulging arm. It pulsated and writhed. Bones cracked and reformed beneath the furred flesh. Konrad needed both hands to grasp Joren's thick wrist. He tried to pin it against the table.

But Joren could be contained no longer. His strength was fearsome, inhuman. In the throes of agony, Joren, more beast than man, did not seem to notice Konrad. The shackles' spikes cut him deeply, matting his fur in blood. He flailed wildly.

With all his might, Konrad tried to force his arm back into the clamp. But it was no use. Joren would not budge.

Then, silence. Joren—or what used to be Joren—stopped moving. His head rocked back. His eyelids fluttered. A large pink canine tongue dangled out of his mouth. His arm went limp.

Slowly, carefully, Konrad dragged it toward the clasp. Centimeter by centimeter, he lugged the dead weight closer. A finger spasmed, its vicious nail slicing lines in the air. Konrad started, choking back a yelp. He almost had Joren secured.

Almost.

Joren's eyes sprang open. His head jerked toward

Konrad, who jumped back in fear. The man-beast, the *werewolf,* glared at him with evil intent.

Its nostrils flared, sucking in air, the beast oblivious to the metal jabbing into its throat. Its lips stretched at their corners, curling back over pink gums, revealing a mouthful of hideous incisors. Konrad thought it was smiling. Then he heard the guttural growl, starting softly but quickly becoming loud enough to invoke caution in proud men. It rose from the beast's throat, sizzled through bared teeth—teeth of a true carnivore, made for tearing muscle and flesh.

The beast was snarling. Its growls insinuated a desire to ravage Konrad piece by piece, to open his belly and gnaw on his guts.

Konrad made one last attempt to drive Joren's wrist into the shackle. It cost him dearly. Sharp, searing pain shot through his chest. With uncanny speed, Joren had lashed out at him. The claws of his freed hand-paw dug deep, ribboning Konrad's shirt and goring canyons across his body.

He fell against the table, howling with pain. The werewolf howled back in mockery.

Konrad checked his wounds. They were gruesome for sure, but not immediately deadly. Had Joren's range not been limited by his binds, Konrad's life would have been forfeited. A centimeter or two deeper, and Joren would have chipped bone and sliced organs.

Though he knew this, Konrad did not feel fortunate. He understood, even then, that the wound would curse him. And that meant Father would—

A shrill howl pierced the air, shaking Konrad in

body and mind. If he did not devise a plan or means of escape, his father would be of no concern.

The werewolf's struggles continued above him. A shackle clanged against the floor. Its freedom could not be far behind.

My dagger! Konrad remembered, fighting through the pain to his hands and knees. He crawled toward the door. Another clang sounded behind him, then another. He scurried faster.

The dagger lay where he had left it, its silver blade shimmering in the lantern light just outside the open door. He crawled toward it, reached for it, and almost had it when the beast grabbed him by his ankle. He screamed in pain, the beast's nails slicing deep into his skin as it lifted him into the air. The beast tossed Konrad as though he was weightless, and he crashed against the wall, falling in a heap upon the floor.

The werewolf was just beginning. It careened toward Konrad like a boulder from a catapult. Konrad scrambled onto his hands and toes and rolled out of the beast's path. He came upon his feet near his bow and quiver.

The werewolf slammed into the wall with a loud crash, nearly taking the entire house down. Pots and utensils fell from the spots on the walls. The beast did not seem harmed, but it was slow to change its trajectory. Konrad seized upon its delay, grabbed his bow and arrows and hurried into the night.

When the werewolf followed, squeezing through a doorway not meant to accommodate its girth, Konrad was waiting. He loosed the first arrow into the beast's chest, a direct hit, though it barely penetrated the demon's thick muscle. The werewolf pulled the arrow from its body and tossed it aside as if it was a minor inconvenience.

Konrad's second shot was even less effective; the werewolf effortlessly swatted it out of the air. Konrad did not get a third shot.

The werewolf leapt off its back paws, propelling itself high into the night sky. It crashed down in front of Konrad. Its long fingers grabbed around his head. Again, Konrad found himself flying. He braced for the impact.

He hit the cold, damp earth with a soft thud. His bow was no longer in his hand and his arrows were strewn about the grass. Out of the corner of his eye, Konrad saw the werewolf leap. He rolled like a log until he found his belly and pushed himself up to his feet.

Again, the werewolf was slow to turn. Konrad rushed toward his dagger. Instead, he ran straight into the beast, who had pounced directly into his path.

The werewolf rose on its hind legs, standing like a man. Konrad gazed up, way up, at a towering, slobbering horror.

The beast stood thrice as tall as Konrad. It began to circle him, dropping back down to all fours. Its loathsome snarling fumed hot breath that smelled of corpses and plague. Here, it would swat at Konrad. There, it would gnash at nothing beside him. It was baiting him, toying with him before making the kill.

As he came full circle back to the threshold, Konrad's foot brushed against his dagger. The beast swiped half-heartedly at his head, and Konrad easily ducked it. While he was crouching, he picked up his blade.

When Konrad drew it before him, the werewolf seemed amused. It swatted at Konrad's hand, but he pulled it back in time. The two continued to circle. Each time it swiped, the beast bared its chest, an opening if Konrad had the courage to take it. The beast clearly thought nothing of him despite his silver dagger. He was a plaything to discard after use, an appetizer before the main course.

Konrad let his mind return to that night one month ago, the night he heard beasts like Joren—no, beasts *including* Joren—devouring his mother. He let himself remember, and he let himself feel it. He remembered his heartache. He remembered his dread. But most of all, he remembered his howling mad desire for revenge.

His mind went blank, filled only with the reds and blacks of raw emotion. His body acted on instinct, some inherent mechanism for self-preservation. He lunged at the monster, his dagger raised. And he thrust it with all of his might.

A fierce backhand sent him soaring into the front of the house. On impact, the air rushed from his body. His vision wavered between blurred light and eternal darkness. He struggled to maintain consciousness, so he could see his end come. He prayed it would be swift.

The werewolf loomed over him. It clutched at its chest and the dagger's hilt extending from it. The beast fell to its knees, its eyes no longer vibrant but dull and hopeless. Its hair receded. Its fangs shrank, square human teeth appearing where Father had spared them.

Soon, only Joren remained. His expression showed only astonishment, shock in knowing that a weak little boy had bested him. His mouth dropped open as if to speak, but nothing came out. He fell over, dead.

Konrad gave up his own fight with the waking world. Darkness took him prisoner, sweeping away the kindness of light.

13.

THE SOUND OF HOOVES hitting dirt, a horse driven to its full potential, stirred Konrad from uneasy rest. His head rang, dull bell-tower tones. He rubbed his temples. Stinging hurt resonated from his chest as his tattered shirt ripped free from blood-clotted cavities.

A horse neighed nearby. *Vulkan.* He struggled for clarity, but his vision would not cooperate. A blurred body lay four meters away. Konrad's dagger lay beside it. He went for it.

"My God!" His father said, dismounting. He looked as if he had taken a stroll through hell.

"I rode as fast as I could." His gaze shifted from Joren's corpse to Konrad, who crouched near the body. "I killed two with ease, all things considered, but the third escaped. He was a strong one, the alpha. I had to hunt him down. You would not believe . . ."

Father's voice trailed off. Konrad stood. He saw no sense in hiding it any longer.

"You have been hurt?" Father asked. The words themselves trembled. Konrad nodded.

"Then I truly am too late." Father raised his arms and approached his son. "Forgive me," he begged, his voice breaking. "Forgive me, son."

Eyes downcast, Konrad listened to his father's display without any affection of his own. He remained still, as dead inside as the man who lay at his feet.

Father took him into his arms, held him close—warmth unreciprocated.

"I will free you from this awful curse, son. Before you turn. Before you kill. God will accept you, I know it. God will—"

Father lurched. The words caught in his throat. He looked down at the dagger in his stomach, right where Konrad had stuck it.

"This is for Mother," Konrad said, pushing the dagger in deeper. He twisted the hilt. "And this is for me."

Father staggered forward and began to cough. He covered his mouth with his hand. Blood sprayed onto it. His eyes widened with fear and confusion, like a deer's after having been pierced with a slightly off target arrow: good enough to kill, but not quickly.

He draped over Konrad, who propped him up just long enough to see his life fading, then tossed him aside. As blood filled Father's lung, the coughing became wheezing. More blood drizzled down his chin and spattered upon the earth. There, Konrad left him to die.

The moon was still high, just beginning its descent. A stiff breeze rattled the trees. The forest beckoned to him, the smell of pine and mud and crystalline waters calling him home. He stepped toward Vulkan, but the horse whinnied and trotted away. Konrad grunted. A sharp tooth bit into his lip, and he curled over himself, his chest racked with pain.

His body screamed for what seemed like an eternity. When the agony dissipated, his chest had healed. His muscles were strong, stronger than they had ever been, alive and alert, just like the rest of him.

Sniffing the air, he caught a pleasing aroma: the smell of hot blood, pulsing through veins. He carried on, into the woods, one foot in front of another, all four feet on the ground.

***

Author's Note

The author would like to thank Abigail Grace, Gregor Xane, Evans Light, and Kimberly Yerina for their advice, insights, and editing contributions to this tale.

"I was alone first in the pack . . ."

You guys are my wolf pack.

About the Author

In his head, JASON PARENT lives in many places, but in the real world, he calls New England his home. The region offers an abundance of settings for his writing and many wonderful places in which to write them. He currently resides in Southeastern Massachusetts with his cuddly corgi named Calypso. He is the author of the novels *Seeing Evil*, *What Hides Within* and many published short stories.

Website:
authorjasonparent.com

Facebook:
www.facebook.com/AuthorJasonParent

Twitter:
twitter.com/AuthorJasParent

Made in the USA
Middletown, DE
28 May 2016